Hedg[e]
Tal[e]

GW00857420

For Jonathan and Peter

Copyright © 1984 Pat Wynnejones

Published by
Lion Publishing plc
Sandy Lane West, Littlemore, Oxford, England
ISBN 0 85648 597 7 (cased edition)
ISBN 0 7459 1489 6 (paperback edition)
Lion Publishing Corporation
1705 Hubbard Avenue, Batavia, Illinois 60510, USA
ISBN 0 85648 597 7 (cased edition)
ISBN 0 7459 1489 6 (paperback edition)
Albatross Books Pty Ltd
PO Box 320, Sutherland, NSW 2232, Australia
ISBN 0 86760 489 1 (cased edition)
ISBN 0 7324 0000 7 (paperback edition)

First edition 1984
Reprinted 1985, 1987
First paperback edition 1989
Reprinted 1992

All rights reserved

Printed and bound in Singapore

THE STORY OF

Jeremy Cricket

Retold by Pat Wynnejones
from Mrs Gatty's 'Parables of Nature'

Illustrated by Sandra Fernandez

A LION BOOK
Oxford · Batavia · Sydney

Nowadays it is very unusual to find an open hearth with a blazing fire where the children can gather round, sitting on a rug in the firelight and looking for castles and palaces in the dancing flames.

And that is why it is now so rare to hear a cricket chirping. For the cricket loves to make his home on a cosy hearth where the flames leap. And he loves to hear the chattering of children's voices.

His country cousin, the grasshopper, loves the wide fields and waving grasses and if you go for a country walk in the high noon of summer you may still hear the grasshoppers chirping their carefree song.

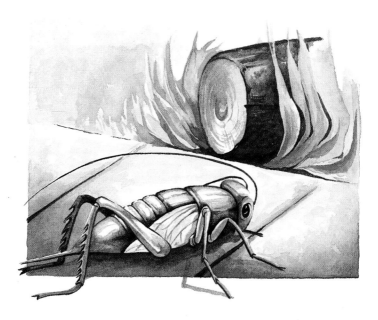

Poor Jeremy Cricket could find nowhere to live — no real little home of his own.

For a while he shared a corner of the woodshed with a friendly spider. Jeremy told the spider how much he longed for a place of his very own.

'It's a sort of tingly feeling in my heart,' he explained.

The spider who was spinning his web with great care and effort seemed to ignore him, so Jeremy tried again. 'The birds have their nests and the foxes have their holes. Moles have tunnels and you have this beautiful web. But I have nowhere, nowhere, nowhere to call home.'

The spider, though friendly, had firm ideas about how people should behave.

'You shouldn't grumble,' he scolded. 'You've been spoilt, I see, and you're discontented. Why don't you go and hop about in the fields with your cousins, the grasshoppers?'

But, deep inside, Jeremy knew that the fields were not the right place for him. He didn't feel happy in the wide open spaces. He longed for somewhere cosy and secure, somewhere safe and bright and warm.

So he said goodbye to the spider and set off to look for it.

One day Jeremy met a young bee, busily collecting honey from the clover flowers in the grass. So he told the bee his problem.

'Why don't you come along with me?' buzzed the bee. 'I'm sure we could find room for you in the hive. Maybe you could be a drone?'

Jeremy thanked him and followed his flight to the hive. But when he saw the busy bees, each one knowing exactly what he had to do and doing it as best he could, Jeremy was anxious.

'It's not the right place,' he said. 'I could never be happy here. There's too much going on. It makes my head spin.'

So he thanked the bee and wandered on.

Jeremy had not gone far when an ant carrying a large white object nearly knocked him over.

'Whatever are you doing?' demanded the angry ant. 'Standing in the way and blocking the path. Can't you see I'm in a hurry?'

'I'm sorry,' murmured Jeremy humbly 'But can't you see, I'm looking for a home. Can you help me?'

'The anthill's back there,' and the ant jerked his head in the direction, nearly losing his precious burden. 'You can go and ask. But you'll have to learn to move faster.'

Jeremy set off with high hopes but when he found the anthill he did not like it at all. Ants were scurrying here and there at a tremendous pace. They whizzed past in front of him and dashed along behind him and came at him from all sides and chivvied him.

'I can't stand this,' he thought. 'It's no home. It makes my eyes water.'

So Jeremy sat down to recover among the short grass and harebells on the slope of a hill.

He listened to the lark singing overhead and watched the small blue butterflies. He could see a cottage in the valley below, but he did not know what it was.

Suddenly there was an upheaval in the ground near him, rather like a small earthquake. There was a gruffling, snuffling noise and then a velvety black nose appeared through the hole. It was the mole.

'What is the matter?' he asked the cricket. 'You don't look very happy.'

So Jeremy explained once again that he was looking for the right place for his home.

The wise old mole listened quietly and thought for a long time.

At last he said, 'Moles make tunnels in the ground; larks soar high in the sky; bees make honey. There's usually a reason, you know. In fact,' he added in his deep gruff voice, 'I'd say there's a reason for everything in the world. Wait and see. There will be a place for you. Everything will be perfect at last.'

Jeremy was grateful for the mole's wise words and he decided to go to his cousin the grasshopper and ask his advice.

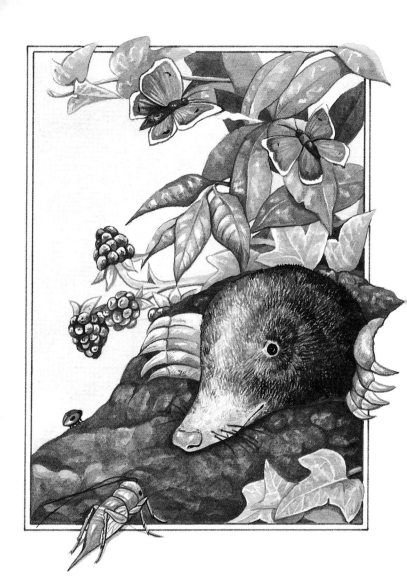

He soon found the grasshopper by his cheerful chittering, but it was quite difficult to make him listen. Every now and then the grasshopper would make a great leap into the air. He had a tender heart and was very musical, but he simply could not stand still. Every time he touched the ground Jeremy managed to say a few words, but it was a difficult conversation.

'So you can't find the right place?' twittered the grasshopper rather impatiently. 'Sure you're not being rather fussy? Seems to me you must think you're pretty special. Why don't you (and up he went, high in the air) come and dance with us? It's great out here in the meadow.'

And up he went again.

'It just doesn't seem to be my place,' said Jeremy, uncomfortable. 'Perhaps there's a reason,' he added, remembering the mole's words.

'Well, I'll examine your joints and legs. Perhaps there's something wrong with them. Just sit on that stone, there's a good chap, and stick your legs out.'

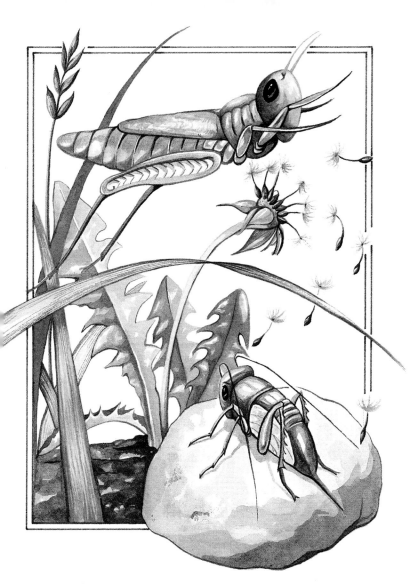

Jeremy did as he was told. He perched on the edge of the stone with his spindly legs sticking out in front of him while the grasshopper carefully felt them over, fidgeting about and jumping up and down all the time.

When he had finished he danced a few steps before giving his opinion.

'No reason,' he pronounced in his squeaky voice, 'no reason at all. There's nothing wrong with your legs — no reason why you shouldn't be dancing with us.'

He did an extra big fidget.

'Oh dear, oh dear — excuse me. I've got pins and needles in my left leg from staying so still. I must be off...' And with three huge leaps he was out of sight.

Jeremy sat on his stone, feeling rather stunned.

'I'm glad he's gone,' he murmured to himself. 'He made me dizzy. He wouldn't know a home if he saw one.'

So Jeremy continued his search for a long time. At last he came back to the hill slope. It was evening. He sat watching the sun go down in a fiery sunset and he saw the first star twinkle overhead.

'Maybe there's no such place as I imagine — warm and bright and safe,' he thought to himself.

Suddenly the ground beside him heaved and broke and up came his friend, the mole.

'I haven't found a home,' Jeremy told him. 'The worst of it is that everybody seems to think I'm making a fuss about nothing.'

'Don't listen to them,' was the mole's reply. 'There's reasons why caterpillars lay eggs on cabbages and robins sing through the winter. There's always reasons. There's got to be a reason for that tingly feeling in your heart. Wait and see. Everything will be perfect at last.'

While they were talking Jeremy began to sniff. There was a lovely smell in the evening air and it was making the tingly feeling very powerful. It was woodsmoke.

Jeremy noticed a curl of smoke rising from the chimney of the cottage below. It was irresistible, and, entranced, Jeremy made his way down the shadowy hill to the cottage.

He hopped onto the doorstep where a blaze of light from the fire streamed under the door, and soon he was chirping on the hearth, safe and bright and warm.

Jeremy had found his heart's true home at last.

The four stories in 'Hedgerow Tales' have been retold from Mrs Gatty's 'Parables of Nature', first published in 1855. Mrs Gatty was a children's writer, and also a keen naturalist, who used stories from the world of nature to illustrate and communicate truth about God and his purposes. Each of the stories has a particular theme, based on a verse from the New Testament of the Bible.

'The Story of Jeremy Cricket' is about 'the heart's true home' of the Christian — heaven. The theme of the story is based on words from the Letter to the Hebrews: 'The world is not our home, but we wait for one which is to come.' (Hebrews 13:14)